HYENAS

HYENAS

JOE R. LANSDALE

Subterranean Press 2011

First Edition

Limited Edition
978-1-59606-355-6

Trade Hardcover
978-1-59606-356-3

Subterranean Press
PO Box 190106
Burton, MI 48519

www.subterraneanpress.com

*For Keith, my son, and a
Hap and Leonard fan.*

HYENAS

THE HYENAS ARE HUNGRY—THEY HOWL FOR FOOD.
KING SOLOMON'S MINES, H. RIDER HAGGARD

WHEN I DROVE over to the night club, Leonard was sitting on the curb holding a bloody rag to his head. Two police cruisers were parked just down from where he sat. One of the cops, Jane Bowden, a stout woman with her blonde hair tied back, was standing by Leonard. I knew her a little. She was a friend of my girlfriend Brett. There was a guy stretched out in the parking lot on his back.

I parked and walked over, glanced at the man on the ground.

He didn't look so good, like a poisoned insect on its way out. His eyes, which could be barely seen through the swelling, were roaming around in his head like maybe they were about to go down a drain. His mouth was bloody, but no bloodier than his nose and cheekbones. He was missing teeth. I knew that because quite a few of them were on his chest, like Chiclets he had spat out. I saw what looked like a chunk of his hair lying nearby. The parking lot light made the hunk of blond hair appear bronze. He was missing a shoe. I saw it just under one of the cop cars. It was still tied.

I went over and tried not to look too grim or too happy. Truth was I didn't know how to play it, because I didn't know the situation. I didn't know who had started what, and why?

Jane had called and told me to come down to the BIG FROG CLUB because Leonard was in trouble. Since she didn't say he was in jail, I was thinking positive on the way over.

When Leonard saw me, he said, "Hey, Hap."

"Hey," I said. I looked at Jane. "Well, what happened?"

"It's a little complicated," Jane said. "Seems Leonard here was in the club, and one of the guys said something, and Leonard said something, and then the two guys inside—"

"Inside?"

"You'll immediately know who they are if you go in the club. One of them actually had his head shoved through the sheet rock, and the other guy got his hair parted with a chair. He's behind the bar taking a nap."

"Ouch."

"That's what he said," Jane said.

"So...I hate to ask... But how bad a trouble is Leonard in?"

"There's paperwork, and that puts me off of him," Jane said, "but everyone says the three guys started it, and Leonard ended it, and well, there were three of them and one of him."

"How come this one is out in the parking lot?" I said, pointing to the fellow with his teeth on his chest.

Leonard looked over at me, but didn't say anything. Sometimes he knew when to keep his mouth shut, but you could put those times on the head of a pin and have enough left over to engrave the first page of The King James Bible and a couple of fart jokes.

"Reason that guy's here, and the other two are inside," Jane said, "is he could run faster."

"But not fast enough?" I said.

"That's where we got a little problem. You see, that guy, he's knocked out so hard his astral self took a trip to somewhere far away. Maybe interplanetary. He's really out of here, and he hasn't shown signs of reentry."

No sooner had she said that than an ambulance pulled up. A guy and a woman got out and went over and looked at the guy on the ground. The male attendant said, "I guess clubbing doesn't agree with him."

"Either kind of clubbing didn't agree with him," the female EMT said.

It took me a minute to get what she meant. To do their job, I guess you have to have a sense of humor, lame as it might be.

They looked him over where he lay, and I was glad to hear him come around. He said something that sounded like a whale farting underwater, and then he said, "Nigger," quite clearly.

Leonard said, "I can hear that, motherfucker."

The guy went silent.

They loaded him in the ambulance.

"Don't forget his shoe," I said, pointing at it. But they didn't pay me any mind. Hell, they worked for the city.

"We got a bit of a problem here," Jane said. "You see, once this guy ran for it, and Leonard chased him, it couldn't quite be called self-defense."

"I didn't want him to come back," Leonard said. "I was chasing him down because I was in fear of my life."

"Uh huh," Jane said.

"He turned on me when I caught up with him," Leonard said.

"Just be quiet, Leonard," she said. "Things will go better. You see, the part that's hard to reconcile, as we in the law business say, is Leonard turning him around, and then beating him like a bongo drum. Leonard grabbed him by the throat and hit him a lot."

"A few times," Leonard said. "He called me nigger."

"You called him asshole," Jane said. "That's what the witnesses said."

"He started it," Leonard said. "And there's that whole deep cultural wound associated with the word nigger, and me being black and all. That's how it is. Look it up."

"No joke," she said. "You're black?"

"To the bone," Leonard said.

Jane turned her attention back to me. "A guy watching all this," she pointed to a fellow standing over by the open door of the club, "he said Leonard hit that guy a lot."

"Define a lot," I said.

"After the nose was broke and the cheek bones were crushed, and that's just my analysis, Leonard set about knocking out his teeth, said while he was doing it, according to the gentleman over there, and I quote, 'all the better to suck dick with, you son-of-a-bitch', unquote."

"So, Leonard's going to jail?"

"What Leonard has going for him, is yon man in yon ambulance—"

I looked to see it drive off with the lights on, but it wasn't speeding and there wasn't any siren.

"—hit Leonard with a chair first, and he did call him the Nigger word."

"You mean the N word. When you say Nigger word, well, you've said nigger."

"Did I say the Nigger word instead of the N word?"

"You did."

"If you're quoting someone said Nigger, isn't that different?"

"I think so."

"Hey," Leonard said. "Sitting right here."

"Well, hell, I've pulled two shifts," Jane said. "Another hour on the job and I'll be calling everybody sweetie baby. Anyway, back to Leonard. Somewhere between the N word, and him chasing the track star out into the lot, he hit one of the other attackers with a chair and slammed the other guy's head into the wall. Ralph, that's my partner, he's in there right now trying to get the fellow's head out of the wall without breaking something. Either wall or victim."

"Actually," I said, "Leonard had to have been provoked. He's normally very sweet."

"No shit?" Jane said.

"No shit."

"I don't think so. But here's what we're going to do. You bring Leonard by the station tomorrow morning, not the crack of dawn, but before lunch, and we'll fill out some papers. I won't be there. I'll be snoozing. But I got my notes and I got statements, and I'm going to turn those in, so they'll be there. And, just as a side note, I really did enjoy seeing that fellow's head stuck in the wall. Before you go, you need to go in there and take a peek, if they haven't got his head loose. They haven't, then you don't want to miss this. It's a fucking classic."

I DID TAKE a look inside the BIG FROG CLUB before I drove Leonard home, and the cop trying to work the guy's head out of the sheet rock was snickering. He looked at me and lost it, made a spitting sound, and let go of him and wandered off bent over and hooting.

Another cop, smiling, went over, and without a whole lot of conviction, pulled one of the guy's ears—the other one wasn't visible—said, "Come on out, now."

The guy's head was pretty far through the wall. It was poking into a bathroom. He must have turned his back to escape and found a wall, and then Leonard shoved the back of his head, pushing the front of it through the wall and into the bathroom. He was all scratched up, like a cat had been sharpening its claws on his face.

The bathroom walls had never really been laid out, just sheet rocked, so it hadn't been too hard to push the guy's head through. I took a good look at him. His chin had locked behind a support board, and the back of his head was locked behind another. He had fit in there easily enough, but in such a way he couldn't get out, and the cops didn't seem to be working that hard to release him.

I said, "You had some antlers, we could just leave you there and tell folks you're a deer."

"Fuck you," he said, but it was weak and without conviction, so I didn't take offense.

I used the urinal, which was just under him and smiled as I peed. I didn't flush. I went back in the main room and saw the back of the guy. He was bent slightly with his butt in the air, standing on his tip toes, probably getting a good bracing from the piss in the urinal.

I went over to the bar, leaned and peeked over. The other guy Leonard had hit was awake and had his back against the bar. A broken chair was on the floor next to him.

I said, "You put your dick in a bee hive, my friend."

"Tell me about it," he said. "We was just funnin'."

"Yeah, how fun was it?"

"Not so much," he said.

I got Leonard and drove him home.

WHEN WE WERE at my place, I sat Leonard in a chair in the kitchen. Brett, my gorgeous redhead, came downstairs. She was wearing a pair of my pajamas and she looked cute in them, as they were over-sized. She was barefoot and her red painted toe nails stood out like miniature Easter eggs. She came over and looked at Leonard.

"Anyone check you over?" she said.

"Wouldn't let them," he said.

Brett made him move his hand and the bloody rag. She checked out the wound. She's a nurse, so she was the right one to do it.

"It's not as bad as it looks," she said. "I think you can get by without stitches."

"Yeah, well, it feels bad," Leonard said.

"Would some vanilla cookies and cold milk make it feel better?" she said.

"Hell, yeah," Leonard said. "Maybe after the milk, a Dr Pepper."

"That can be arranged," Brett said, "but first, come in the bathroom and let me patch you up."

When that was finished, Leonard came in with a bandage on his head. Brett got him a plate with some cookies on it and a big glass of cold milk. Leonard sat and smiled and dipped the cookies in the milk.

I said, "So, what happened?"

"They called me a queer."

"You are a queer," I said.

"It was their tone of voice," he said.

"How did they know?" Brett said.

"I made a very delicate pass at one of them," Leonard said.

"How delicate?" I asked.

"I merely asked him if he was gay, because he looked it, and then the shit hit the fan."

"Actually, you hit a guy with a chair, shoved another guy's head through some sheet rock, and beat the cold dead dog shit out of the other guy in the parking lot. No fan was involved."

"Yeah, that was pretty much it," Leonard said, and bit into a cookie.

NEXT MORNING WE went down to the cop shop. They sent us in to see the chief. He was in his office. There was a cop I had never seen before in there with him. They had a bunch of photos spread out on the desk, and the cop was laughing.

I glanced at the photos. They were of the guy with his head through the sheet rock.

The cop was trying to get hold of himself, trying to quit laughing.

The chief said, "You can't act professional, you can just leave."

The cop went past us and out of the room. He was giggling as he went, trying to hold it in, making a sound like a kid spitting water.

"Have a seat," said the chief.

There were two chairs on our side and we took them. The chief said, "We can't have this, fellows. It's keeping all my officers from doing their jobs. They keep coming in here to look at the crime scene photos."

He held up one of the photos.

It was of the guy's face thrust through the sheet rock.

"This one," he said, "is especially precious."

I made the spitting water sound the cop had made.

"And then," he said, "there's this one."

This was an extreme close up of the fellow's face, casting a baleful eye out at us.

The chief even laughed this time. He put the photo down on the desk.

"Everyone in the department had copies made. Officer Jane Bowden took them, in the name of efficiency and coverage of a crime scene."

"Do you have any wallet size?" I asked.

"No, but we're having some made up. Listen here, Leonard. You're lucky. Witnesses said they started it and you had to defend yourself. Bar owner is pressing charges against them. Thing is, them starting it, that's probably right, but sometimes, it don't hurt to walk away."

"It was the chair upside my head kept me from walking," Leonard said. "It knocked me down for a minute, and then when I got up, I was perturbed."

"Point taken," said the chief. "Not only were there witnesses, but one of the three you whipped is a witness himself. In your favor. He's going to have to pay a fine and some repairs at the club, but he's admitting they started it."

"Which one would that be," Leonard said. "Mr. Sheetrock?"

"No."

"I'm betting it isn't toothless," I said.

"That would be a good bet."

"So, that leaves the one I knocked over the bar with a chair," Leonard said.

"Bingo."

WHEN WE WENT out, we saw the guy who had been knocked behind the bar. He was sitting in the waiting room. He hadn't been there when we came in.

Leonard touched two fingers to the edge of his eyebrow in salute as we passed.

The guy was about thirty, blond, and in good shape. He might be nice looking when he healed up. His left eye was closed and swollen and black, his lips were red and meaty like rubber fishing worms. As he followed us out into the parking lot, he had a limp.

We were about to get in my car when he came toward us.

Leonard turned, said, "You and me not finished?"

The man held up his hands. "We are. Mr. Pine—that's right isn't it? Pine?"

Leonard nodded.

"I want to apologize," the man said.

"Accepted," Leonard said. "Good bye."

"Wait. Please."

I had been at the driver's side, about to get in, but now I went around on Leonard's side and we both leaned against the car.

"My name is Kelly Smith. I want to hire you." He was looking at Leonard when he said it.

"Hire me?" Leonard said. "What for? You like to take beatings?"

"Nothing like that. I have this problem. That's why I was at the bar."

"Drinking problem?" I said.

"No," he said, looking at me. "And who are you?"

"A friend," I said.

He nodded, spoke to Leonard. "Could we talk private?"

"You got something to say, say it," Leonard said. "Me and Hap can hear it together and no one will cry. We're not criers."

"I don't know," I said. "There was that movie. You know the one."

"Oh, *The Last Airbender*," Leonard said. "Yeah. That sucked. That could make anyone cry. And what was up with that Three-D? It should have been in Smell-o-vision."

Kelly stood there while we went through our act. When we finished he said, "What I need is someone to do something tough that's a little against the law."

"How little?" Leonard asked.

"Well," he said, "maybe a lot more than a little."

WE WENT TO a coffee place and got a table near the back wall. There was music playing, and there were a few people at tables, and a nice looking woman in very short shorts came in. Never been a fan of the heat, but for some things, you had to love summer.

Leonard said, "Hap, pay attention."

"Right with you," I said.

"I'll tell Brett," he said.

"I'm back, just watching the scenery, not trying to move it around."

Kelly had been looking at her too. Now he looked at us. He said, "I wasn't really with those guys last night."

"Sure looked a lot like you," Leonard said.

"I know," Kelly said. "I meant they aren't friends."

"You fought like they were your buddies," Leonard said.

"We didn't fight well," he said. "You kind of walked through us."

"I staggered a little," Leonard said. "That chair hurt."

"You went down and you came up like a jack in the box," Kelly said. "When you did that, I thought you were fucking Dracula."

"Actually, I would have been Blacula. Ever see that old movie?"

Kelly shook his head.

"Never mind," Leonard said. "Look, it's nice, you buying us coffee and a Danish—"

"I'm having an apple fritter," I said.

"Okay," Leonard said. "Danish and fritters, but if you've got something to say besides I'm sorry and let me buy you coffee, then let's move on. Me and Hap are busy men. We got places to go, things to do, and people to see."

"Not really," I said. "Our day is pretty open."

Leonard gave me a sour face.

"I'll pay you to help me out," Kelly said.

"We talking about moving a piano?" Leonard said.

"No," he said. "We're talking about maybe you having to rough someone up."

"First off," Leonard said. "Why? And how much?"

"It's my brother, Donnie. He's in deep doo-doo," Kelly said.

"What kind of doo-doo?" I asked.

"He got in with these fellas that rob armored cars," Kelly said.

We all sat there for a moment and let that statement hang between us like a carcass.

"This is starting to sound like doo-doo that's too deep," I said.

"It's deep all right," Kelly said. "He's only twenty-one. Good kid, really."

"Except for wanting to rob an armored car," I said. "I would consider that possibly a blemish on his character."

Kelly nodded.

I said, "He's twenty-one, you're like, what thirty? You guys are some years apart, aren't you?"

"Thirty-one, and yeah, he was like a surprise," Kelly said. "Dad wasn't all that good about hanging around anyway, but that little surprise, Donnie, it was more than he could handle. He took the car out for an oil change, and just kept going."

"So what's this got to do with me?" Leonard asked.

"You know that robbery took place in LaBorde last year, the armored car guards at the bank?"

"Yeah, I remember," Leonard said. "They got the guards when they were transporting the money out of the bank to the truck. Just walked up with masks on and had guns and locked the guards in the back of the truck. It was maybe, what, two hundred thousand dollars they got?"

"About four hundred thousand," Kelly said. "They must have had someone waiting that drove up, picked them up and took them away. No one knows. All they know is they were there with Halloween masks on one minute, then they had the money, and then they were gone. That was it. Took the guard's guns and put the guards in the back of the armored car and put plastic cuffs on them. Fastened one cuff to their left ankle, one to their right wrist. Then had them put an arm behind their back and fixed it there and pulled the plastic down to the other ankle, linked it from behind. That way they couldn't move well, damn sure couldn't run."

"That's cute," I said.

"Was your brother one of them?" Leonard asked.

"No, but I think he's about to be."

"And, pray tell, why do you think that?" I asked.

"Because in his room he's got some articles about the heist," he said.

"That doesn't mean anything," Leonard said. "Hap has books about Satan, but he ain't a Satanist. At least, as far as we know."

"Those damn books and that rap music," I said. "They can change a man."

Kelly ignored me. Sometimes it's all you can do. He said, "Yeah, but Donny, he has these friends come around, and they lock themselves in the back room for hours. I know they're smoking dope. I can smell it. But what I really worry about is I think these friends are the robbers and they want to pull my brother in."

"That's a big guess," I said. "Any reason to have it?"

"These guys, they're a real tough bunch," Kelly said. "And as you can tell, I'm not so tough."

"You take a good fall, though," Leonard said.

"You still don't have any serious reason we should believe your brother is about to be part of a robbery."

"I heard them talking. I was sort of sneaking around, and I heard them say they needed a driver. The guy talking was the one Donny calls Smoke Stack. That's the name they all call him. I guess cause he smokes all the time. I don't allow it in the house, but he smokes anyway. I asked him not to once, and he just lit up and smiled at me, went in the back room with Donny. Hell, even Donny is tougher than me. He grew up different. He grew up tough. I can almost guarantee you these guys are going to rob another armored car, and they're going to pull Donny into it."

"Still a little lame," I said. "But, if you think you got something, go to the police. We know the chief over there. I'm not sure he likes us, but he did get some humor out of the photos of your buddy with his head through the sheet rock. So right this minute, he sees Leonard as a comedian."

"I go to the police, they're going to run Donny in, and he's a good kid, really. He was living at home, and our Mom died. A heart attack. She was overweight, didn't take care of herself. Went to hell after our dad ran off with another woman and went up North somewhere. She died, I moved back home. But I wasn't able to do it right away. I had a job in Austin, and I had to find another one up this area. I work at the University, doing janitor work."

"What did you do before?" I asked.

"I was a computer specialist, and I made half a mil a year. Now, I got just enough to buy gas for the car and bread for the table. I kind of thought Donny wasn't doing so good and needed me here. Last time I saw him, before Mom died, I could tell he was making some bad decisions. But the bottom line is these friends of his. I don't like them, and I'm sure they're the guys."

"That's your instinct?" I said.

"Yeah."

"Well," Leonard said, "instinct is all right, but it can be you telling yourself something and thinking you're enlightened. Gut instinct tells people to believe lots of things, and most of them are wrong. And, Kelly, this isn't our problem. It's a police problem."

He shook his head. "No. The police pick up Donny, his life is ruined."

"He robs an armored car, a bank, he might get a bullet through his head," Leonard said. "That ruins things too."

"Yeah, that can cut a career short," I said.

"Last night, I went to that bar looking for help. I didn't tell the details to those guys, but I said I was looking for someone could do a little rough house work. Those guys were recommended to me by a fellow I know. And then there was that whole thing about one of them calling you a name, and it all getting started…I think they started it just to show me how tough they were. Next thing I knew, I was in it with them, you know, part of the pack, and then I'm down, and one guy's got his head through the sheet rock, and you're chasing the other guy outside. And you're older than them."

"Watch it," Leonard said.

"All I'm saying is, after I saw that, I decided maybe you were the guy instead of them."

"I don't know," Leonard said.

"Donny, he really looks up to this Smoke Stack. He wants to impress him. The guy's got muscles on muscles and he's just mean. Just mean."

"The gut instinct again?" Leonard said.

"Yeah."

"Well," Leonard said, "in cases like that, the gut is often right. We still know a shark when we see one. That's why we crawled out of the water and became men in the first place. Only thing is, some of the sharks crawled out after us."

"That would be the lawyers," I said.

"I told Smoke Stack and his buddies not to come back, but it doesn't matter," Kelly said. "They come around anyway, and if they don't, Donny goes to meet them. Him being twenty-one, I can't legally tell him squat."

"You wouldn't know where he goes to meet them, would you?" I asked.

"No," Kelly said. "And I'm embarrassed to tell you, I'm afraid to follow. I'm afraid they'll catch me. I think Smoke Stack and those guys would do anything."

"What about the other guys, his pals."

"Three of them. They're followers. It's Smoke Stack runs the program, that's easy to see. I don't know their names, anything about them. Hell, I don't really know anything about Smoke Stack."

"Say we looked into it, found Donny was just smoking dope, or maybe he was selling drugs. What then?"

"I don't know. Maybe you can discourage him. It's such a mess. I wanted to be a big brother to him, but he doesn't care what I think. This Smoke Stack, I think he's like a tough father figure. And he looks like he could wad up a wrench. Again, I think he's like a father for Donny."

"Fathers just need to be tough in will," I said. "It don't hurt if they can bend a tire tool over their knee, but it's not part of the job description."

"Yeah," Kelly said, "but Donny doesn't know that. Look, really. He's a good kid. He's just got to get straight. He gets into this, his life is ruined. I got some money. It's from my savings, saved up before I moved here. I'll give you ten thousand apiece."

I looked at Leonard. He sighed.

I said, "Look, for right now, hang onto your money. Let us think about it, maybe look things over, and then, if we think we can help, we'll talk. If not, we'll still talk. But you might not like the conversation."

"Sure," Kelly said. "Sure, that's all right. That's good."

THAT AFTERNOON, WE went over to the gym to work out. Our gym sucks. It's small and it's hot and it has a small mat room. The mat is thin as paper and smells like sweaty feet. The owner isn't someone who is much into gym work himself. He's a guy with a physique akin to a rubber apple. He sits on a stool by the door so he can get some wind from outside, meaning there's no air conditioning. The door's always open, except dead of winter. Flies are always fluttering about.

He sits there to check memberships. The only advantage his gym has is his memberships are cheap, and he's not that far from the house. The only conversation I remember having with him was him saying, "That'll be thirty dollars a month, apiece."

But, it's all right. We bring our own gloves when we spar. When we spar we use fists a lot, but in real situations I like to use an open hand along with fists.

You can use open hands with the gloves we have, but we're friends, and that kind of business can sometimes be worse than fists. Nothing says, "Oh, shit," like sticking a finger in your buddy's eye.

We moved around a little, flicking punches, throwing kicks. We were gym fighting, not really fighting. The two should never be confused. The first is like a swim in a heated pool, the other is like being dropped into a stormy, shark-infested ocean.

So, we were moving around, getting a work out, popping each other a little, and I said, "You believe him?"

"I don't know," Leonard said, pausing a little, putting his hands on his hips, taking a deep breath. "Maybe. A story like that, it's so stupid it's bound to have some reality about it. I mean, a guy has a problem with his younger brother hanging with thugs that might be bank robbers, so he goes into a bar to get someone to beat the robbers up."

"You think that's all he wanted?"

"I don't know. Maybe he wants us to do something more permanent with these guys."

"That, I don't want to do."

"We may not need to. Here's the thing, Hap. I think the guy is serious about being worried about his brother, but maybe we can look into it and solve it better than him. We don't, he's going to hire someone like that guy I left in the parking lot. Then things will turn messy, and before it's over Kelly and his brother both might go to prison."

"Usually, you're talking me out of stupid shit like this."

"Does it ever work?"

"Not so much. This guy got to you a little, didn't he?"

"A little."

We moved around some more. Leonard hit me a good snap on the forehead. I hooked low, then switched to an overhand right and caught him on the cheek.

He said, "Ouch, I've had enough for the day. That was right on my wound."

"That was your cheek," I said.

"I don't mean the taped part of my head, I mean the bruise. I am so wonderfully black you just can't see it."

"If you say so."

There was no place to take a shower, and as part of our workout, we had jogged from my house, into town and to the gym.

As we jogged back to my place, I said, "We can check into things, see the lay of the land. If it's not lying right, and we don't like it, we can step out. Call the law if we choose."

"Then we'll have some explaining to do."

"We say we thought the guy was full of it, and just wanted us to straighten his brother out."

"You think these guys really are bank robbers?" Leonard said.

"I don't know," I said. "Anything is possible. Say they are robbers. Kid comes along, they see a new recruit. Someone to drive the car is my guess. They start buttering him up with all their King Robber stories, tell him how he'll be rich and his own man, that kind of stuff. The kid, not having a father around and his mother dead, his brother not being around before, maybe not having the relationship they could have had, Donny's ripe for bad business."

"Sure, it could be like that."

We jogged along, silent for awhile. I could tell Leonard was thinking things over, and I let him.

Finally, I said, "So, are we going to check it out?"

"Say we take it easy. We determine if the kid really is in trouble. If these guys really are robbers, and if there's anything we can do about it without getting locked up. I reckon we ought to do that much."

"That's how it is then," I said, and we bumped fists.

WE GOT OUR friend Marvin Hanson to come in with us. He runs a private investigation agency, and he was once a cop. Sometimes we work for him. Last job we did was simple and we didn't get paid because the client didn't like the outcome. He didn't pay Marvin so Marvin couldn't pay us.

Because of that, Marvin owed us a favor.

We had him meet Kelly. We had him watch Kelly and Donny's house, see where the kid went, and when he went, and if he went with some guys that looked tough.

When he finished a shift, I took over, and then Leonard took over. We had been at this for a couple of days. We were posted down from the house twenty-four seven, near an empty soccer field with grown up grass and missing goal nets.

So, it was Marvin's watch, and I was home with Brett, and we were upstairs in bed reading, and Leonard was snoozing on the couch downstairs, having finished his shift watching Kelly's place not too long back. I put the Western I was reading down, glanced at the clock. Twelve midnight.

I was about to turn in, get some sleep before I went on at eight a.m., and the door bell dinged. I don't like it when the door bell dings that late.

I got my automatic out of the drawer by the night stand, and Brett got her revolver.

"I'll check," I said. "Leonard's down there, and if it's anything nasty, you call the cops."

I went downstairs, but the door was already open. Leonard was letting in Marvin.

I said, "Man, that was a short shift."

"Yeah," Marvin said.

Marvin has a limp and a cane. He was quick to find a chair. He took off his hat, which had once belonged to a friend of ours, and rested it on his knee. He said, "Things went a way I thought maybe you ought to know about."

"SO, ABOUT NINE-THIRTY I'm sitting in the car, thinking I'd like to be home in bed with the wife, when I see a car pull up at the curb. Four guys get out. One of them looks like he lifts weights. Lots of weights, big weights, heavy weights."

"That would be the loveable Smoke Stack."

"Yeah, for all that muscle business, he's smoking like the proverbial smoke stack."

"Oh, Marvin," I said. "That is good. Him smoking like a smoke stack and having the name Smoke Stack. You are so clever."

"Yep. They go around back, and then coming back from around the house I see all of them again, and this younger guy that I figure is Donny. They got in the car, tight as coins in a miser's wallet, and drive away. I followed. They went out to the warehouse district, and I went with them, but sneaky-like. They never saw me. They went down where the rentals are. It's one of those cheap places. No cameras, no security gate. You just drive in and take your padlock off your shed. I couldn't follow them in, so I drove across the street and looked. I could see through the fence and I could see them park, and I could see which storage building they opened. I could see a car in there. An older car, a muscle car. Something that could run like a spotted ass ape if needed."

"Ah, the old spotted ass ape," Leonard said. "How fast do they run?"

"They are very fast," Marvin said. "So, they're there awhile with the door pulled shut, and I could see they had a light on because it was shining under a crack at the bottom of the door."

"That is some of that ace detective work you're famous for," I said.

"My guess is, if they're planning a robbery, that storage shed is their villains' lair."

"Probably has a basement in there, test tubes and shit," Leonard said. "It's like the evil Fortress of Solitude."

"I got another guess too," Marvin said. "When the other robbery went down, the one with the guards, about a month later they found a guy in a car out in the woods with a bullet through his head. He'd been dead for awhile. At the time it was unexplained. Just a random murder. But, I been thinking maybe the dead guy was their getaway man. And when he got them away, they put him away. My guess is Donny is next on the list. They get some young guy doesn't know squat, they use him for the robbery, for the driving, then they pop him and the cut is bigger. Next time they got plans, they recruit again. Each new driver doesn't know about the other. It works until the word gets out they're finding lots of dead people in stolen cars with false license plates."

"So Donny is just a tool for them to use and then destroy," I said.

"That's my guess. Another thing, I followed them after they left the warehouse. They didn't take

Donny home. They drove him to a house on the edge of town. Most of the block there is burned out, and beyond it the town quits and the woods start. It's a rundown place where the back acres have been sawed over by pulp wood workers. I parked there for a little while, then drove to the warehouse and got closer to the building they were in. It's number fifteen. Then I came here. I could go back and finish my shift, but I don't know I need to now."

"Probably not," I said. "We know where they keep the getaway car, and we know where they live. And that they may have sold pulp wood."

"That pulp wood money could be the way they financed the first robbery," Marvin said. "Bought the getaway car. Now they got money from the first robbery to pull another. They aren't living high on the hog out there, so they're keeping what loot they got tamped down for now, which is smart."

"Marvin," I said, "your work is done."

"So we're even on what I owe you two?" he said.

"We are," I said.

"Good luck to you," Marvin said, got up and picked up his hat and cane. "If you need me for anything, even or not, give me a call."

Marvin went out and closed the door.

I looked up and saw Brett was sitting on the top stair looking down, listening. I smiled at her and she waved. She was wearing those oversized pajamas and my bunny slippers with the ears on them.

She said, "How about we have some milk and cookies?"

"Hell, yeah," Leonard said.

WE SAT AT the kitchen table and had our milk and vanilla cookies and thought on the matter. Way we saw it, if we waited until they decided to rob an armored car it would be too late.

First off, we didn't know when they had their little heist planned, and we didn't know if they might tire of Donny and pop him. We didn't even know if they were actually the robbers, but it sure seemed likely, and we were going to play it that way.

We thought about a number of cool ways to go at it, and we explained them to Brett, and she said, "Why don't you just go over and confront them, tell Donny how things went with their past driver. Otherwise, while you're making your plans, he could already be the wheel man and dead and under some log in a creek somewhere."

"There's a logic to that," I said.

"And it fits what you've done in the past," Brett said.

"You mean strong-armed our way through?" Leonard said.

"Yeah," Brett said. "You guys are smart enough, but you don't have the patience to be masterminds."

"Yeah," Leonard said, "and it's boring, and yucky, and I don't want to do it."

"So there," I said. "If we go over, confront them, and if we convince and save Donny, they could still commit the crime and they could kill another idiot driver. I know that's not supposed to be our problem. Our problem is supposed to be just Donny, but I don't like it."

"If you convince Donny to leave," Brett said, "then you can give an anonymous tip about the car, say it's stolen or something, because most likely it is, and put the cops on it."

"They'll need more proof than that to go take a look," Leonard said.

Brett crossed a pajama clothed leg, dangled a rabbit shoe from her foot, picked up her glass of milk and sipped. When she sat the glass down, she had a thick, beaded, white milk mustache that made me smile.

"That's right," Brett said, "they will need more proof, but that tip could start movement in the right direction. After that, you get stuck on what to do, just come to me and I'll figure it out from there."

NEXT DAY WE went over to the University and drove around for awhile before we could find a visitor's parking spot that wasn't filled, and walked over to the building where Kelly worked as a janitor. On the bottom floor students moved about and an older woman in a janitor's uniform was pushing a trash cart. She looked about as excited as a corpse.

We asked her about Kelly, and what she told us sent us by elevator to the fourth floor. Leonard wanted to push the button, and I had to let him, or I would never hear the end of it. He likes pushing buttons on elevators. I can't explain it. But, every time he gets to do it, for several minutes afterward, I must admit, I feel slightly deprived.

There were no students on the top floor. I went to one of the windows and looked out. I had gone to the university for awhile. I had been a good student. I enjoyed it. I still liked the atmosphere of a university, but I was too lazy to finish up my education, and most likely the classes I'd taken long ago in stalking the wooly mammoth and how to build a fire with flint and steel and a gust of wind, were no longer valid.

We looked around a while and found an open door and heard some clattering, went in there and discovered Kelly banging a garbage can against the inside of his cart so it would empty.

Kelly looked up at us. The swelling around his eyes had gone down. He said, "You wouldn't believe the stuff you find in these cans."

I leaned my ass into the desk up front, and Leonard took a seat at one of the standard desks in the front row. Kelly put the garbage can back in place by the teacher's desk, said, "Well."

"We reckon you're right," Leonard said. "Those people Donny is running with, they're not up to any good, and that means neither is Donny."

"Can you do something about it?"

"Maybe," I said. "But here's the thing. We do what we're talking about doing, you might not be safe. You might not want to go home for awhile."

"How long's awhile?"

I shook my head.

"I see," he said. "And you can get Donny out of this?"

"You can't make a man believe what he doesn't want to believe," I said. "But we can try and show Donny that things aren't as good as he might think. In fact, they're really worse than we thought."

"How?" Kelly asked.

We told him about the dead man in the car, what we suspected. When we finished, Kelly found a desk and sat down. He said, "Shit, how does stuff like this happen?"

"Humans," I said.

"Yeah," Leonard said, "they can be pesky."

"So," I said, "What we're asking is, do we go ahead with things? Cause if we do, it might make it hot around the old hacienda. Meaning, you need to not be there. And the job here, I don't know how safe it keeps you."

Donny nodded slowly. "I got some place I can go for awhile. I mean, I can figure that out. But the job, I need this job. I need it bad. I can't just walk away."

"We can't guarantee your safety, you stay on the job," I said. "We don't recommend it. We didn't have any trouble getting to you, and if they decide to find you, it won't just be to talk."

"I'll leave the house," Kelly said. "But I'll stay with the job. Go ahead and do what you need to do."

"We'll need a photo of Donny," I said.

"I can do that, after work," Kelly said. "But, you will try to save him, won't you?"

"We'll do what we can," Leonard said, "and more often than not, that's a lot."

MARVIN WAS OUT of it now, and we didn't work in shifts after that. We just drove over together and parked down the street from where Kelly lived. Every now and then we would move the car to a new position, so no one in a house nearby would call the law on us.

Kelly had followed our advice and found a new place to stay. We told him not to tell us where. That way we didn't have information we didn't need and wouldn't want to accidentally spill.

We also had something else. A last gift from Marvin. Having been a former cop, he had good connections. He got us information on Smoke Stack. Once he knew where he lived, and what his car license was, it wasn't so hard. Marvin wasn't sure about the other guys, but he was sure about Smoke Stack. The license led to the car, and that led to a description, and that led to a rap sheet. I had that with me. And a grainy photo that had been faxed to Marvin and that he gave to us. Smoke Stack's real name was Trey Manton.

Leonard had a small flashlight on and he was using it to look the photo over again and read the rap sheet. We had already done that, but it was a way to pass the time. Leonard spent a lot of time looking at the bad photo. He clicked off the light and closed the folder and put it on the seat between us, said, "Man, that guy looks like he tried to roller skate in a buffalo herd."

"I'm going to guess the buffalo may not have turned out so well. And he's done time for drugs, and he is, shall we say, a violent person, as his prison time shows."

"We are violent ourselves," Leonard said. "But we're the good guys."

"I guess that's one way of looking at it," I said.

"Rather us as tough guys, than people like Smoke Stack as tough guys."

"And yet another way of looking at it."

Leonard gave me Smoke Stack's photo. I looked at it again just to have something to do. I gave it back, and took the photo of Donny and looked it over. He looked like the usual, pimple-faced, sassy ass kid. It was a full body shot, and it made me think of the photos I'd seen of Billy the Kid, only without the cowboy hat, the rifle and the six gun on his hip. But it had the same attitude about it. The rifle and six gun had been replaced by sagging pants and tennis shoes that looked too big for his feet. The strings were untied. That's showing them.

As it got dark and they didn't show up, we decided to go to their place and have a chat. Maybe Donny was already with them. With Kelly gone, maybe he no longer saw a need to go home. Next thing was they'd move into Kelly's house and never let him come back. They were the type. I had seen it before.

When we got over to the address Marvin had given us, we parked down from their house in the lot of an abandoned convenience store. It was about three blocks from their house, but seemed the best place to park. Everything there was as Marvin said. The houses and most of the convenience store were burned out and you could smell the dead fire still. Something had set the whole block on fire. Where the burned buildings ended, the woods took over, and up on a hill with some logged out acres behind it, was the house.

I opened the glove box and got out my automatic and gave Leonard his. They were both in black holsters, but the guns themselves did not match. Brett thought it would be cute if we got matching guns with our initials on them.

We got out of the car and Leonard pulled out his shirt and lifted it up and clipped on his holster. He arranged his shirt around it. It was only hidden if you weren't looking for it or you were blind in one eye and couldn't see out the other. I clipped mine to my belt. I was wearing a loose tee-shirt, so it didn't cover much.

"Ready?" I said.

"I was born ready," Leonard said.

"Scared?"

"I never get scared."

"Bullshit."

"Okay, I'm a little scared. Let's get it done before I get more scared."

We started walking.

THE HOUSE HAD a car out front, and we had to climb up the hill to get there. We stayed to the right side where there was still a line of trees just behind a barbed wire fence, and then there was a pasture, and more trees, and then the house with the logged out area behind it.

The house was not well lit and there wasn't much you could tell about it in the dark, but there seemed to be a sadness that came from it. All old uncared for houses seem that way to me. As if they are living things dying slowly from neglect. It's like they're old people no one will visit, or if they do, it's out of obligation or even spite.

There were a series of walking stones that led from a place near the road to the front porch, but grass had mostly covered them. There were a few shingles lying like scales in the yard; they had blown off the roof in a high wind. The rest of the yard had grass growing tall enough to hide a rhinoceros if he crouched a little. There was a washing machine in the yard, tipped on its side, and it looked to have been a popular model about the turn of the century. An old stone bird feeder was still standing. Grass seeds had gotten in it along with enough blown dirt and dust to make a bed, and blades of grass had grown up in a manner that made it look as if someone had used Butch Wax on them.

There was a thin beam of light escaping from under a window to the right of the door. I went up and bent down and looked through the window. There were three guys on the couch passing a joint back and forth. The light of a television strobed across their faces. One of them was Smoke Stack. He was hard to miss. He took up about a third of the couch. He was wearing a tee-shirt with the sleeves rolled up so folks could get a look at his biceps, which looked like bowling balls in tight rubber tubing. There were tattoos on his arms, some kind of Chinese writing. I figured Smoke Stack was doing well to read English, let alone Chinese. The tats looked like they had been made by a blow torch and a fountain pen.

I didn't see Donny.

I stepped back and Leonard took my place. After he took a look, he said, "Rock and roll."

I went up on the porch and Leonard went around back. We didn't say that we should do this. We just knew it. It wasn't our first rodeo.

I carefully pulled back the screen, which had so many holes punched through it, it might as well have just been a frame. It squeaked a little, like a dog toy.

I waited. No one shot at me through the door. No one jerked the door open. I could hear the TV. It was some kind of music show. Music videos, I guess. The music playing was Rap, the only kind of music I can't stand, unless it's bag pipe music, which, with the exception of "Amazing Grace," always sounds to me like someone starting up a lawn mower.

I heard the back door breaking open, and when I did, I kicked the front door with all my might. It hurt my foot a little, but the door sagged back, which spoke not so much for my manliness as it did for the geriatric state of the house.

Rushing inside, I had my gun drawn. I was wearing my bad ass smile. I know it's bad ass because I practice it in front of a mirror.

AS WE CAME in, me from the front, Leonard from the back, I focused on the three on the couch. As I said, one of them was Smoke Stack. The thugs on either side of him were almost interchangeable. Lanky with pot bellies and greasy hair, arms branded with tattoos, their heads wreathed in cigarette smoke. They looked like the kind of guys that might share a brain, and today the brain had a day off.

Sitting in chairs to the side were Donny and another guy. Leonard was watching them. Donny looked like a dumb kid, thin faced, big-eyed, his chin bristling with a few hairs and competing pimples. The guy next to him was dark and short and stout and sunburned. He had his hair cut in a military 'do, probably because the hair on top was as thin as dirty water. Overall, he gave the impression of someone who had lived on a planet with heavy gravity and too much sunlight.

They jumped up and went for guns they had in their pants. Except Donny. He just sat there with his mouth hanging open.

Leonard waved his gun, said, "Who do I shoot first?"

There were no volunteers. They stopped moving.

I had my gun pointed too. I said, "Okay, boys, let's keep standing, and take them out one at a time, starting with you, Smoke Stack. Put them on the floor. And I'm not talking about your dicks."

"Do I know you?" Smoke Stack said.

"No," I said. "But you're about to know a little about me, and my guess is you aren't going to like it."

When they had the guns on the floor, I told them to kick them lightly away. Leonard held his gun on them, collected theirs and took them outside. I watched through the open door as he threw them under the porch and came back inside.

"Nice night," I said to no one in particular.

Leonard turned off the TV.

"What you guys want?" Smoke Stack said. "We ain't got nothing for you to rob."

"I think maybe you got some money from a bank robbery somewhere," Leonard said.

Smoke Stack looked at Leonard, then me, then they all looked at Donny. They just kept staring, like they were waiting for him to break out into a little dance.

"No, man," Donny said. "I didn't tell them anything. I don't even know these guys."

"He ain't lying," I said. "He doesn't know us. But, we are here for Donny's benefit. We want that you should quit this group, Donny. Come home and quit acting like a gangster wannabe. Or what we refer to in the privacies of our homes as a dumb dick."

"My brother," Donny said. "He sent you. That's it, isn't it? Well, he and you both can keep your nose out of my business."

"Just come home and forget these guys," I said. "You do that, life will be a lot better for you, and so will the air. Man, you guys could use a bath. Or is it because you're shitting behind the couch."

"Ha!" Smoke Stack said. He looked at us and our guns like he was looking at kids with suckers. "You ain't so much."

"We got guns," I said. "That puts us way ahead of you. We took yours away from you. And you know what? We might not give it back."

Smoke Stack looked at Donny. "Who are these guys, kid?"

"I tell you, I ain't had nothin' to do with them. I tell you, I don't know these guys."

"They know you," he said.

"Actually, we know who he is," I said. "He doesn't know us, and we don't know him. But we have a nice photograph. And we know this: You are planning to pull a heist, and the kid here, you want to get him in on it, and then when it's over, you'll pop him, and we're not talking about with a wet towel."

Smoke Stack let that revelation roam around in his head for awhile. It went on for so long you could see it cross behind his eyes, like someone moving past a window. I glanced at Donny. There was something roaming around in his head as well. Suspicion I hoped.

"What the hell you talking about?" Smoke Stack said.

"That doesn't sound all that convincing," I said. "The part where you try to act like you don't know what's going on, and you've don't remember how you clowns shot your last wheel man and left him in the woods for the ants."

"What's he talking about?" Donny said, looking at Smoke Stack.

"They don't know nothing," Smoke Stack said. "They're just talking air. Don't pay them no mind. You really don't know them, then just keep your mouth shut."

"What they like to do," Leonard said, looking right at Donny, "is they hire some dumb ass to drive their car, and then they kill him and split it between themselves."

"What, for one less split we kill a guy?" Smoke Stack said.

"Yep," I said. "And, hey, you fellas, what makes you think one of you isn't next? Were you all in on the previous job? Are there some bodies in the woods somewhere?"

I could tell from the way a couple guys looked at Smoke Stack that I had hit a chord.

"You guys don't listen to this shit," Smoke Stack said. "And you, Donny. Ain't I treated you right? I been more of brother to you than your own brother."

"You mean you've kind of let him do what he wants," I said, "because at the bottom of it all, you don't care about him. He's just a pawn. It's tough being a father or mother or big brother, cause they got to tell you stuff you don't want to hear, make you do stuff you don't want to do. But you, you can just tell him everything's all right, even when it isn't."

"I ain't got to do nothing," Donny said. "My brother, he ain't much of a man."

"And Smoke Stack is?" I said. "Your brother works his ass off for you. Butt wipe here steals what he wants and hangs out. Not a whole lot of manly in that."

"I could snap you like a stick," Smoke Stack said.

"No," I said. "No, you couldn't."

"You talk tough with a gun," Donny said. "I've seen what he can do. You ain't so tough."

"What?" Leonard said, grinning at Donny. "Smoke Stack? Tough? With some drunk, maybe? Some poor guy half in the bag. You think he's bad because he has muscles and tattoos and cigarette breath. Hap here, on his worst day, could turn him inside out and make him say how much he likes it."

"Ha!" Smoke Stack said.

I went over and gave Leonard my gun. Now he had one in either hand. I took off my jacket, hung it over the door knob of the door I'd kicked open.

"Why don't I show you that he's not so tough," I said.

"That'll be the goddamn day," Smoke Stack said.

"This is, in fact, that day," Leonard said.

Smoke Stack grinned at Leonard. "I get through mopping the floor with him, you're next, nigger."

"Oh, don't make me wet," Leonard said, then he waved the guns at the others. "All you assholes, except Smoke Stack, and you Donny, all of you over here and on your bellies. Make like fucking run-over snakes."

They did what they were told. They lay on the floor on their bellies by the wall, lifted their heads up to see what was going on.

Leonard looked at them, said, "All you dick cheeses, all you move is your heads, savvy? Donny, you sit on the couch. You get a bird's eye view."

"Why we doing this?" Smoke Stack said.

"Because we can," I said. "And because you think you're tough as an old saddle."

"You're too old for me," Smoke Stack said to me.

"Yeah, well, I'll try not to hurt you too bad."

"I think tough guy is starting to waffle, Hap," Leonard said. "I think he's looking for a hole to run into."

Smoke Stack said to me, "We get started, it goes bad for you, your man will step in with the guns."

"He's got the guns to keep your friends in line. It goes bad for me, I'll take my beating, and then we'll leave."

"Shit," Donny said. "Think you can beat Smoke Stack, you're crazy. I seen him whip two guys once, and one of them with a board."

I felt a little nervous right then, because that old adage about how bullies are always cowards isn't true. Sometimes they're bullies simply because they can do what they say they can do, and they enjoy doing it.

Leonard said, "Yeah, but it ain't how many guys he whipped, it's the guys. Hap, he wasn't one of those guys."

"He whips Smoke Stack, hell, I'll go with you," Donny said. "That's how much faith I got in him."

Smoke Stack looked at the kid and nodded.

"All right," I said. "I don't whip him. You stay, and we'll go, and we're out of your life. You rob banks, you fuck goats, you do what you like. We're done."

"You'll be saying stuff to folks you shouldn't, like we're going to rob a bank," Smoke Stack said. "We wouldn't want people believing something like that. You ain't got no proof of nothing that way."

"We'll make it simple for you," Leonard said. "You whip Hap, we'll leave, and then, so you don't cry at night, you can always come and try to kill us before we let the cat out of the bag. We'll give you a whole two days. You got our word, and that's better than yours, I'm sure."

"I whip him," Smoke Stack said, nodding at me, "then I'm coming for you. That's gonna be a treat."

"You don't even know me," Leonard said, then smiled at him. "And you don't want to. But if Hap slips on a banana peel, then I'll put the gun away, and me and you can dance all over this place."

"Hey, Smoke Stack," I said. "You gonna talk us to death, or you gonna show me what you got."

There was a clearing between the people on the floor and the couch where Donny sat. Leonard was by the open door, pointing the guns. Smoke Stack moved forward, and as he did he crouched a little and put his fists up. He smiled at me, came closer.

He hooked a big right. I could have seen it coming with a bag over my head. I stepped into him at an angle and the punch went around me. I popped a jab in Smoke Stack's eye, hooked him to the throat. He had his chin down, so the hook was a so-so shot. Still, he didn't like it. He stepped back with a sputter, coughed a little, and came at me windmilling. I leaned way right when he was right on me, put out my foot and caught his ankle as he rushed. It catapulted him forward and into the wall and caused him to knock a hole in the sheet rock with his head, then to roll on top of his gang members.

When he got himself straight and turned, I kicked Smoke Stack in the balls so hard people in China had heart pains. I stepped in quick and gave him a left hand three stooge poke in the eyes, hit him with a right cross that came from hell without a bus ticket and that smacked against the ridge of his jaw. He twisted and went down and started to get up, but didn't.

"You waitin' on reinforcements, Smoke Stack?" I said.

"What he needs to get up," Leonard said, "is a fucking winch truck."

Smoke Stack finally got upright, rushed me with his head down, bellowing like a bull. I hooked my arm under his neck as he came and went back on my hips and kicked him in the nuts again and lifted him over me so that he hit hard on his back on the floor. I could hear the breath go out of him, loud as an elephant fart.

I flipped back so that I landed straddling him, slammed my forearm into his nose and chin. Once. Twice. Three times.

He quit struggling. I got up and looked down at him. His face was bloody. He rolled over on his stomach and started crawling away, like a roach that had had its rear end stepped on. Then he collapsed, quit crawling. He was unconscious.

Donny was looking at me with his mouth open so wide you could have turned a semi truck around in there.

Donny said, "Did you kill him?"

"Just his pride," I said. "And maybe one of the two brain cells he had. That leaves him one so he knows how not to shit himself. Now, come on."

Donny looked at Smoke Stack, then at me. "I don't know."

"We had a deal. You can come, or Leonard here will pistol whip the goddamn shit out of you and we'll take you anyway. You can go without knots and bruises, or we can fix you up. You get to choose. And you get to choose right now."

Donny nodded.

"We'll be taking all your guns," Leonard said. "We're gonna make Donny crawl under the porch and bring them out. He's going to do that without pulling one, so that way we don't have to shoot him. You can check for your pistols at the bottom of assorted lakes, creeks and rivers. And if you follow us, I will personally shoot holes in your head and when they find you, your guns will be shoved up your asses."

WHEN WE WERE in the car, Donny seated in back, said, "But he was so much bigger."

"David and Goliath," I said. "Ever read that passage in the Bible?"

"No. What's it mean?"

"It means David got lucky," I said.

"Only Hap wasn't lucky," Leonard said. "He was skilled. Smoke Stack, he's got big arms and a big mouth, but he was gonna get you killed, kid. We done you a favor, and you don't even know it."

"I don't believe that," Donny said, but his voice didn't hold a lot of conviction.

"Yeah, well, you can be stupid, or you can be lucky, and right now, you're goddamn lucky," Leonard said.

"I didn't think anyone could do that to Smoke Stack," Donny said.

"Your problem, kid," Leonard said, "is you haven't been doing a whole lot of thinkin', just reactin', and you hadn't been around long enough to know life ain't like the movies. I get the whole lost-your-parents thing. Been there. But that don't have to turn you stupid. That's a choice, like wearing green stretch pants. You don't have to do it."

"My brother shouldn't have done this," he said. "He shouldn't have asked you guys to do this."

"Woulda, shoulda, coulda," I said. "We're trying to save you from yourself. But, we got a time limit, boy. You fuck it up later, then we done what we could. You can go back to being stupid and probably shot to death in a car out in the woods. But, for right now, we got other plans."

"What plans?" Donny said.

"Pancakes," Leonard said.

WE WENT TO my place and made pancakes. It was late by the time we did, and Brett came in. She was carrying a newspaper. She saw Donny sitting at the kitchen table with a large glass of milk and a plate of pancakes covered in syrup. He was eating heartily. Leonard sat across from him with a Dr Pepper. Leonard thought Dr Pepper went with most anything. Brett nodded at Leonard and Donny, said to me, "So, you found a child in the yard and took him in to raise."

"Found him under a rock," I said. "Can we keep him? We'll build him a pen out back."

She smiled at me. "We'll think it over. You got any more pancake batter?"

"Coming right up, banana pancakes," I said. "I should work at IHOP I'm so good at this."

I went about making her pancakes. While I did, she sat at the table and looked at Leonard for an explanation. Leonard told her all about it.

Brett looked at Donny, said, "Honey, you could have been in some real trouble."

"I just wanted to make some money." he said, and the way he looked at her it was hard to determine if he was seeing a sister figure, a mother, or someone he wished he was old enough to date. Brett had that effect on people.

"So taking someone else's money is okay so you can have some?" she said.

"Smoke Stack said it's not someone's money if they can't keep it," Donny said. "And besides, that's bank money, it's insured."

"Someone pays out the insurance, baby boy," she said, "and that might be me if I bank there." She picked up the newspaper and hit him a pretty good whack in the back of the head. "Bad dog. Bad, bad dog."

Donny lowered his eyes, said, "I didn't think about it like that."

"You haven't been thinking," she said. "You been hearing some bullshit, is what you been hearing, and I got to say, for you to take it as fact, you must want to believe it. There's people born stupid, but you're one of those Hap calls the Happily Stupid. They believe what they hear, not what they investigate or think about. They're the ones that don't listen to news, they listen to opinions and editorials and think it's news. Rumors and lies and sometimes the truth. It's all the same to them."

"I haven't had it so good," Donny said.

"So, you're like a special case?" Leonard said.

"Ain't no one matters but yourself," Donny said. "That's what Smoke Stack told me."

"Then that means you don't matter much to him," I said. "He's telling you the truth when it comes to his philosophy. He doesn't care about you or anyone else. You're just a cog in the machine, and he wouldn't mind replacing you with another cog at the drop of a hat."

I put Brett's pancakes in front of her and heated up the syrup a little in the microwave. I brought it to her and then got her a cold glass of milk. I sat down across from her.

When I sat, I put my hands in front of me, clasped together, and Brett said, "You okay, Hap?"

"I cut my knuckles."

I held them out for her to see.

"So you did."

"I think I can use some sympathy."

"We'll talk about it when we go to bed," Brett said.

WHAT WE ENDED up doing was not going to bed right away, but calling Marvin, and getting him out of bed, and pissing him off, but he came over anyway. He came over with the information about the body found in the woods, and in fact, he had gotten a copy of a photograph from one his cop friends, had it in a big yellow envelope. We didn't look at it right away.

Once he had some of my pancakes, his attitude was better. We went into the living room, and Marvin told Donny some of what he knew. He took the photo out of the envelope and showed it to Donny. It was a clear photo of a man behind the wheel of a car. He had a hole in his forehead, and he was swollen up so bad his shirt collar had rolled into the swell of his neck. Insects had been at him, and a string of ants were clearly visible crawling into his nose.

"No gun was found," Marvin said. "He didn't shoot himself."

"That could be anyone at anytime," Donny said.

"Yeah, it could," Marvin said. "It's a possibility it is someone unrelated to your buddy Smoke Stack. It could be a pumpkin painted up to look like a man. But I don't think so. Timing's right, the description of the car fits."

"There's lots of cars like that one," Donny said.

"You got me there, kid. You're bound and determined to get yourself killed. So have at it. You want to take the chance it's not connected, that's your bailiwick. Me, I'm going home."

Marvin stood up, leaving the photograph on the coffee table.

On his way out, Marvin picked his hat and cane off the back of a chair, said, "Nice knowing you, kid. Next time I see you, it'll be in a photograph like that one."

Marvin went out and closed the door.

"Bullshit," Donny said.

"He's just trying to help," Brett said.

"He's trying to scare me," Donny said.

"Yeah," I said, "he is. I hope it's working. You damn well better be scared. This is some serious business we're talking about. Smoke Stack, he's a loser. He's so cool and important, why's he live in that shithole and have a bunch of other losers hanging around him, and that includes you. But it doesn't have to."

"He does all right," Donny said.

"Yeah," Leonard said. "Well, he don't keep his left hand up worth a shit."

"Or his right," I said.

THAT NIGHT WE put Donny in the little guest bedroom we had built for Leonard. It wasn't very big, but we had built it onto the back of the house. There was a window that Donny could climb out of if he were ambitious. The only thing was, Leonard was sleeping in the bed under the window and near the door. Donny was sleeping on a pallet on the floor. Donny would have had to have been a Ninja to get out that window and Leonard not know it.

As we walked him to the bedroom and I laid out his pallet, Brett brought him pajamas and a towel for a shower, Leonard said, "I'm a light sleeper. And if you wake me up, thinking you're going to sneak out. I'm going to beat the hell out of you. That's as simple as I can put it."

Donny looked at me.

"He will," I said.

"Here," Brett said, handing him the towel and pajamas. "Baby, you ought to listen to these boys. They know what they're talking about. Like your brother, they just want to help you."

"My brother is a loser," Donny said.

"Your brother quit a good job to come here and take care of you," Leonard said. "He went from high living to low living. He's a janitor. Good honest work, but not work of his choosing. He did that for you. He may not be perfect, but he did it for you. That means something."

Donny didn't say anything to that.

Brett said, "You should listen. Those people you were with, hell, not people... Those beasts you were with. They aren't human. They're hyenas. They might have been people once, but they're hyenas now. You don't have to be one too. You get to choose. That's the difference between you and a natural born hyena. There's a choice for you. For the animal there isn't, but for humans to choose not to be animals, there is."

"Actually," Leonard said, "I like the hyenas better than humans."

"I don't know what you mean," Donny said.

"That's what scares us," I said.

"He knows," Brett said, and took hold of Donny's chin with her thumb and forefinger. "He's just not ready to admit it... And Donny, honey, be sure and take that shower before you lay down to sleep. You'll sleep better, and you won't stink."

Donny looked as if someone had just stuck a hot shot to his balls.

"Not trying to hurt your feelings," Brett said, "just fact. Girls sure don't want to be around some stinker. And you're kind of cute, if you'd clean yourself up."

"Really?" Donny said.

"Really."

"Smoke Stack said if you got money, you got the girls."

"Did he?" Brett said. "That's like saying if you got corn you get the pigs. Thing is, who wants pigs? Look here, kid. Get a shower, and let's see we can do something about those pimples. You just aren't washing your face good. And I got some stuff you can put on them. Even a natural beauty, a goddamn goddess like me sometimes gets a bump."

NEXT MORNING BRETT slept in, and I went downstairs and woke Leonard and Donny. I called Kelly and told him we had his little brother, and that we would try and hang onto him for a few days, to see if common sense soaked in. I didn't offer him any guarantees.

We called Marvin about seeing if he could drop a word to the police about the car in the shed, and so on. He did. They didn't really have enough cause, but they went out and cut the lock anyway. The car inside was gone. The place was empty. They went out to the house where Smoke Stack lived. It was cleaned up and only Smoke Stack was home. He told them the bruises on his face were from falling down in the driveway.

It was an iffy move, putting them on the alert like that, but me and Leonard figured it was best to make them a little nervous.

After we got the news, Leonard said, "Smoke Stack and his swinging dick friends are done tidying up. There's nothing left for the cops to find. I think we should have shot them all last night. I think we should have shot Smoke Stack twice."

Donny was sitting on the couch listening.

"That includes you," Leonard said.

"He's just testy," I said. "He hasn't had his morning coffee. And his boyfriend isn't talking to him."

"You're gay?" Donny said to Leonard.

"Yep."

"You don't act gay."

"How do they act?"

"I don't know…"

"Look here, kid. We come in all shapes, sizes, and attitudes. But it's pretty much a given we all have big dicks."

"Yeah," I said, "but he doesn't have an ounce of fashion sense."

"No Barbara Streisand records either," Leonard said. "I just prefer men to women. And just for the record, I can whip your ass and pretty much anyone else's on any day of the week, provided the Moon is in Leo."

"What?" Donny said.

"He's fucking with you," I said. "About the moon in Leo part."

We went to the gym and took Donny with us. When we got there we put the bag gloves on him and showed him how to work the heavy bag. He didn't want to do it at first, but Leonard persuaded him with a threat. After Donny hit the bag a few times, he got into it. He started asking questions on how to throw punches. He had seen us do it, seen how we moved the bag, and he wanted to learn it. I think he was also thinking about that ass-whipping I had given his hero.

Leonard said, "You got to come from the hip. But, you get older, you get more experience, you realize this bag don't mean shit. Hitting a person, you don't have to be able to move this bag. You got to hit a man when he's in the void, when he's stepping, when he's trying to shift or recover his balance. Catch him them, you can take down a big guy with a simple punch, a kick. Catching someone off balance, or controlling their balance, makes them easier to throw."

We spent two hours at the gym, then went back home.

We pulled up in the drive, and I saw the front door was open. Leonard and I were in the front seat. He turned and looked over his shoulder, said, "Donny, you stay in the car. If anyone comes out shooting, or you hear shooting, you run like a motherfucker. But, you don't hear shooting, I come out, and you're gone, I will track you down—"

"And beat the shit out of me," Donny said.

"That's right."

We had guns in the glove box and we got them out. Leonard went around back, and I went up on the porch and moved the open front door wider with my foot, peeked inside.

I didn't see anyone. I moved in slowly, and then I heard the back door lock click, and Leonard was in.

Leonard took the kitchen, and I took his room. We checked the bathrooms. I went upstairs. The bed covers were pulled back and the big red tee-shirt she had slept in was lying on the floor. On the end of the bed was a note.

I picked it up and read it.

We got your redhead. We got Donny's brother. We got your lady's cell phone, and we got your number. Go to the cops, they're both dead. Wait for our call.

THERE'S NO WAY to describe the emptiness I felt. I went downstairs with the note and gave it to Leonard. He read it and went upstairs and came down with a shotgun, two pistols, and a single shot .22 rifle. None of them are registered. I keep them in a special place in the closet where the ceiling tiles can be moved and the guns can be stored.

I sat at the table, stunned, and Leonard went out and got Donny and brought him in.

Donny looked at me, said, "What's wrong?"

Leonard gave him the note, said, "That's your man, Donny. He's got Brett and your brother. That's what cowards do."

Donny put the note down. "Smoke Stack said no one would get hurt. He said we'd just end up making some money."

"Someone will get hurt all right," Leonard said. "Smoke Stack. And anyone with him. If he hurts Brett, we'll kill them all and shit on their graves on a weekly basis."

"Brett didn't have anything to do with this," Donny said.

"Yeah, and that mattered, didn't it?" Leonard said.

I was thinking on what to do next, when the cell rang.

When I answered, Smoke Stack said, "All right, bad ass. We got your woman and she's going to drive the getaway car for us. That's ironic, ain't it, asshole? It didn't take all that much work to figure who you guys were, cause first off, we got the brother, and, it didn't take more than a few burning cigarettes on his chest, and he talked right up, told us who you were. How you like that?"

"Peachy," I said.

"We nabbed Donny's brother at his job just before he started to clean a toilet. Now listen up tight cause

I ain't gonna repeat it. We hit the First Commercial Bank at 1:30 today. Anyone should get tipped off before then, or at all, we'll kill the chick and the brother too. What we're gonna have the redhead do is drive the getaway car. Ain't that classic? You take our wheel man, and we take your girl, and now she's our wheel man. Pardon my goddamn fucking manners. Wheel woman. I hope she can drive, cause if she can't, got to just go on and pop her."

"She can drive," I said. "Don't hurt her."

"Man, that would be a shame, wouldn't it. Fox like that. She's fine, man. I don't know how you got something like that. I see her, and I see you, I got to wonder you got some kind of Love Potion thing going."

"Just don't hurt her… How do I get her back?"

"You didn't mention getting the brother back. So, we'll keep him. We'll keep him until we're gone for some time. We give the redhead back, you tell who we are, then he's toast. Otherwise, a week from now we'll let him go… No. I don't like that. You see, I'm thinking since you didn't even ask about him, he's not such a big worry for you. You get the woman back, then what do you care? We'll do it the other way. We'll keep the redhead and give you the brother. A week from now, we'll let her go. Just so you know, we caught her sleeping. Just sprang the lock and found her upstairs. I made her change, and I watched while she did it. It's good to know she's a natural redhead. It's good to know what she's got under the hood, so to speak."

"Fuck you," I said.

"Don't get rowdy. It might not do to get me mad. And let me tell you something. Other night, you got lucky. I was high as a kite."

"Yeah, and you can't fight either."

"Maybe we'll get another chance and I can show you what I can do when I'm straight."

"Maybe we will."

"Tell you what. We keep her a week, we'll give her back, but in the meantime, we might try and put out that little fire between her legs. I'm a regular fireman."

"You hurt her, you touch her, you're dead," I said.

"I wouldn't talk like that, if I was you. There's all kinds of things can happen between now and then. You could be looking for her for twenty years, and not so much as find a hair. That body we left in the woods, in the car, that was a mistake. From now on, there won't be bodies to find. So you better pay attention to me. You sit quiet. We'll hit the bank. We'll leave the brother somewhere, and then we'll let your woman go in a week. That way, we got plenty of time to do what we want and get where we want. You don't believe me, call the police. Show up and cause trouble. You might get me, but you won't get her back. Least not alive. Have a nice fucking day, asshole."

I put the cell away and told Leonard what Smoke Stack said.

I said to Donny, "He won't let your brother go, and he won't let Brett go. He knows we know who he is, and he's determined to pull the armored car job anyway. Out of spite. He's trying to prove he's smart."

"I'm so sorry," Donny said. "I guess I haven't been thinking."

"You ought to be sorry, kid," Leonard said. "You've stirred up the goddamn bees' nest."

"He might let them go," Donny said.

"No," I said. "His pride is what this is about. He knows at some point we'll tell somebody, so I figure he'll do the robbery, then tell us he's going to let the brother go, and we can pick him up at such and such a place, but neither brother or Brett will be alive by then. And they'll be waiting for us. They'll ask that you come along, like they're gonna take you back. But you know what? They plan to kill us all. No witnesses, and then they're back in business. Cops will know it's them that did it because of circumstantial evidence, but thinking and proving, that's too different things. They could lay low for a year or two and then launder the money somewhere, come out good. And my figure is everyone in that group, except Smoke Stack, will turn up dead. He'll end up with all the money and no one to talk about how things were done."

"You know, it's not a nice thing to say," Leonard said, looking at Donny, "but this is all your fault."

"It is, isn't it?" Donny said.

"Damn straight," Leonard said.

"It's not all your fault," I said. "I was Kelly, I'd have told too. No one is as tough as they show in the movies. I should have thought that angle. We tried to play this one too nice."

"Hap likes being nice," Leonard said. "Me, I don't care for nice."

"Will you go to the police?" Donny asked.

"We could take that chance, but we won't," I said.

Donny looked at the floor, then up at me. "It's not an armored car this time."

"No?"

"They're just going to hit the bank. Two inside, and then they'll come out and the getaway car will be waiting. I wanted to tell you that. He shouldn't have bothered Kelly and Brett."

"I bet Smoke Stack stays in the car," Leonard said.

"Yeah," Donny said. "Him and one of the others. And the driver."

"And now that driver is Brett, and your brother will be in the car too," Leonard said.

"All right," I said. "That doesn't change much, it might make it easier, no armored car guys to worry with."

"Yeah, it really doesn't matter," Leonard said. "But you showed some balls by telling us, by stepping farther away from that asshole Smoke Stack."

"What will you do?" Donny asked.

"What Leonard said earlier. We'll kill them all and shit on their graves."

IT WAS STILL early in the day. My guess was they would keep Brett and Kelly alive until they were finished with the job. That would be their insurance until they didn't need them anymore. I had to hold onto that idea. It was my only comfort. Still, it wouldn't be long after the job was over that both Brett and Kelly would end up dead.

I called Marvin and told him the situation.

"So, how about I park somewhere where I can see them do the robbery. The asshole even told you the bank."

"He thinks he's untouchable."

"I can be an eyewitness later. Say I saw them. Right after I shoot the living hell out of them."

"Just be a witness," I said. "Don't get involved. Leonard and I will take care of them."

"I know that," Marvin said. "I never thought otherwise. But I can do my part."

"Not for us you won't," I said.

"I didn't say anything about it being for you and Leonard. It's Brett I'm talking about."

"And I appreciate it, but just watch what goes down so you can say you saw them there. If you see us, kind of forget that you did."

"If they call me on the witness stand later and ask if I saw you two?"

"Lie under oath."

"Certainly. I just wanted to make sure we were on the same page."

WE MET MARVIN at a drive-through eatery about noon, had some coffee. I don't remember if I drank mine or not. We were sitting in Marvin's car. Leonard's car was parked beside it. Donny was sitting with us.

"Donny, you stay with Marvin," I said.

"You don't have to worry about me running," Donny said. "I want my brother back. I want you to get Brett back. She was right. I do get to choose."

"Yeah, well," Leonard said, "talk is cheap."

"By the way," I said, "in case you choose wrong, I'm not worrying about you running. Marvin will shoot you."

"I will," Marvin said. "A whole lot."

"Maybe somebody ought to shoot me," Donny said. It was a little dramatic, but right then I think he meant it.

Leonard raised his hand. "Who's for it?"

"Right now you just stay out of trouble, Donny," I said. "This kind of stuff is our business."

"Yeah, like we don't fuck up regularly," Leonard said.

"Not this time," I said.

"But they said for you not to come," Donny said. "That if you did they'd kill her."

"They'll kill her anyway," Marvin said. "So, it's then or not at all."

Leonard and I got in his car. We had put false license plates on it that morning, and we had a roll of false pin stripes to use. It was a stick-on thing you could remove easily, then wipe the sides of the car with some rubbing alcohol and it was like it had never been there. It was a little thing, but it was something that might throw an observer off.

Just to keep the disguise theme going, Leonard and I were going to wear hats.

Marvin was to drive to a spot across from the bank. A hotel parking lot. It would be quite a coincidence, him being at the hotel parking lot at the same time as the robbery, considering he'd turned in information about them earlier. Information that didn't pan out. But, he planned to tell them the hotel had a hell of a catfish buffet, and that he liked to take it in now and again, just happened to be there when the whole thing went down. Donny being there might take a bit more explaining, but in the end, truthfully, I didn't think it would matter. Not with what I had in mind.

We stopped in a lot behind a closed supermarket and got out and quickly put the pin stripes on the car. We put our hats on and drove to a place across the street from the bank. It used to be a mercantile store, but like most things downtown, it had gone the way of the dodo bird. From where we were, we could see the bank and we could see the hotel across the way. Marvin and Donny were parked in the lot.

The little mercantile lot was now a free parking lot, and it was full of cars. Mostly people who worked for the bank. We didn't try to find a parking spot, we just drove to the rear of where all the cars were and pulled up there. As we sat, a police patrol car came by on the street between us and the bank. He didn't look our way. Which was good. I had the .22 bolt action rifle in my lap; it held one shot at a time. In the back seat was a shotgun. We had pistols in the glove box. No land mines or golf clubs.

I opened the door quietly and got out of the car and looked over the roof, and over the roofs of the other cars in the lot. From there I had a clear shot.

I got back in the car.

I looked at my watch. 1:15.

I took a deep breath. Leonard said, "It'll be all right."

"It'll be all right when it's all right," I said.

"We'll get them."

"He could have lied about the time," I said. "He could have done that."

"Yep," Leonard said, "but I think he feels safe. The coward's way is to be brave when he holds the cards. Not when he doesn't."

"I just hope I'm not the one to hurt her."

"Hell, Hap, when was the last time you missed a shot?"

I tried not to remember when that was, tried not to imagine I could miss.

"Listen, brother," Leonard said, "I can do the shooting for you. I'm not like you. You know, in Vietnam I killed a lot of men. The only ones I feel bad about are the ones I tried to kill, shot at and missed. I remember them better than the dead ones cause all I can think about is they may have gone on to kill one of us. I'm not like you. I don't carry the burdens of popping off a bad guy. I can get closer somehow, and I can do it."

"No you can't. You're an all right shot, but when it comes to this business I'm the one to do it. And it needs to be done from as much distance as the shot will allow."

"You got me there."

I nodded. "Yeah. I do."

I never learned to love guns. Didn't sit around and talk about how big a hole they can put in something and from how far. I didn't need bigger, better, and more. I don't enjoy the smell of gun oil, don't even like cleaning them. I don't know all the brand names and all the calibers and such.

But I can shoot a long rifle better than damn near anybody outside of a trained sniper, and I'm okay with a handgun if it's not too extreme a shot. I just have a knack to aim at something and hit it. Put a long gun in my hands and I can normally put a shot up a gnat's ass, and that's without the gnat bending over and pointing to the target.

Right then, however, all I could think about was that I might miss. I had certainly missed before, but I didn't want this to be one of those times.

Leonard knew what I was thinking. He often does. "You won't miss, Hap."

We didn't say another word. Just sat there and watched and listened to each other breathe. I paused once and looked in the mirror on the back of the sun visor. I should note I looked pretty cool in my hat, a brown fedora. Leonard didn't look so sharp in his. He loved hats, but like I keep telling him, he isn't a hat person. Every hat he wears looks like something left on a scarecrow.

1:30 came and they didn't. Had Smoke Stack given me a line of shit? I felt like I was going to burst out crying.

Five minutes later we saw a car with two of the guys that had been with Smoke Stack in the house that night. The skinny, pot-bellied guys.

The car was a replacement for the one they had originally stored in the shed Marvin told us about. A brown, speedy model. They parked it in a slot and sat for a moment. I got out of the car with the .22 and laid it over the roof. I was a good distance away, and I had a limited shot over the roofs of parked cars. My stomach fluttered.

Way I figured, those guys in the brown late model would hit the bank, rush out and into the getaway car as it arrived. Smoke Stack, Brett and Kelly and Stumpy would be in that car. Brett would be at the wheel. When the robbery was done, the others would jump in the getaway car and go. Brett would have to drive them out of there. I hoped like hell she didn't try to get cute, wreck the car. She did, they'd kill her or the wreck might. With Brett, you never knew. She was a fighter.

Way they planned it, if things went wrong with the pick up they had a spare car in the lot. But the best thing was to have a getaway driver waiting so the robbers wouldn't have to start up and back out. It wasn't elaborate. It was simple. Simple was what worked.

The two shit heads got out of the car, ready to go in the bank. They had on gloves and jackets under which I was sure there were guns.

I had the .22 beaded on the back of the head of one of them. A .22 isn't a heavy firing weapon, but it doesn't recoil much and in matters like this, it isn't fire power, it's aim. The .22 had another advantage. It wasn't particularly loud.

I took a deep breath, two more, then slowly let out all my air, steadied the rifle. My face was beaded with sweat and a drop ran into my eye. I wiped it away quickly with my arm. The sweat had spoiled my aim.

They paused, and the one I hadn't sighted talked on his cell phone. That would be the call for the getaway car which would be nearby. And that would be the pause I needed to set my shot again.

They started walking toward the bank entrance. I sighted down the barrel, took three deep breaths again, let out all my air and gently tugged the trigger.

The sound of the shot was like someone snapping a whip. The guy I was aiming at folded his legs under him and sat down quickly like he was about to start meditating. I knew there would be a small hole in the back of his head, but the front would have one the size of a half dollar. There would be a punch out of bone, an explosion of blood and brains on the concrete. As I watched, he leaned forward slowly, his forehead hitting the cement.

The other man with him wheeled and pulled a gun and darted back toward his car. I shot and hit him in the side before he made it. He went down. I could hear him scream from there. He threw the pistol aside and got up on his knees and held both hands up in surrender; he was a professional quitter.

I could tell he hadn't seen me yet, had no idea where the shot had come from. He was rapidly turning his head from left to right, front to back, holding his hands up.

He yelled out to no one in particular, "I haven't got a gun. I give up. I quit."

All I could think about was Brett.

I timed the turn of his head and shot him between the eyes. He fell back. I tossed the .22 in the backseat and climbed back in the car. About that time, people came out of the bank. They gathered around the bodies.

We sat where we were. People were looking in all directions. I took deep breaths and let them out.

"Easy," Leonard said. "Two down."

Then we saw a black SUV pull into the lot.

Brett was at the wheel. Smoke Stack was beside her. One of the other shits was in the back; the one Smoke Stack called Stumpy. I didn't see Kelly.

I GOT OUT of the car again with the .22, keeping it held down low. But when Smoke Stack saw the situation at the bank, the crowd, his boys down in the lot, he had Brett drive on. Nothing speedy. She just eased out of the lot. So far, no one even knew the SUV was supposed to be part of what was going on.

I was sure neither Smoke Stack or Stumpy had seen me. I got in the car and we eased out of the lot with our hats pulled down low, and followed the SUV.

It went slow as it turned down the street toward the square, and then it hit South Street and turned. Holding a ways back, but not too far.

My cell rang. I answered.

It was Marvin. "You on them?" he asked.

"On them," I said.

They went along for a few lights, driving casual, then they turned on highway 7. We pulled down a little dirt road and got out and pulled off the pin striping and threw it and our hats into the bushes. It was most likely wasted energy, but it was the only clever thing we had had time to plan, and frankly, it wasn't that damn clever.

We got back in the car and went after them, finally caught up and stayed behind them at a goodly distance. Another car passed and got between us. But that was all right. It was a kind of camouflage. We all three drove out highway 7.

We went on for quite some time, and then the car between us turned off, and we fell back a little. There was road work ahead, and they fanned the SUV through, but stopped us. We sat there and waited. It was a cool day, but I was sweating. They were getting ahead of us.

"Should we run it?" I said.

"Stay cool," Leonard said.

That was like asking a polar bear to stay cool in Albuquerque in mid-July.

Finally they waved us through. Leonard put his foot to the floor. We didn't see them. We had lost them.

I CALLED MARVIN.

"Man, we lost them. We're gonna need you out here to help look. We got to do back roads. Shit, I don't know what we got to do."

"Take it easy," Marvin said.

"Easier said than done. Goddamn road work. It got us hung up."

"Where are you?"

"Out Highway Seven."

"Highway Seven. We're coming... Wait. Donny. He wants to talk to you."

"Fuck him."

"It's about where they might be."

"Then put him on."

"Hap," Donny said, "I want to help."

"Then you better not be wasting my time with a chat."

"Smoke Stack, if he's out Highway Seven, he's going to The Take Off. That's what he calls a pasture out there. I think his family might have owned it. It's about twenty acres, used to be a hay field, has some aluminum buildings. He keeps an Ultra-light there. That's why he calls it The Take Off. He uses the pasture as a kind of airport. He could be going there. I was there with him once. Went out to help him get a car from one of the sheds. One we had stored for the getaway, before you found out about it. He could have stored the car back there."

"For a trade off?"

"Maybe. But that's a place he could be. Maybe they're just hiding out there. I don't know. But it makes sense."

He gave me the directions. It was down a county road. We had passed it. Leonard wheeled the car and we drove back.

THE PLACE WASN'T hard to find, not once we knew which road to take. Donny explained all that over the phone. There was a line of trees, and then a pasture. From the directions, we concluded we were at the right place.

We parked by a small bridge. I spoke into the cell. "We're here."

"Good luck," Donny said.

"Luck has got nothing to do with it," I said, and turned off the phone.

I took the .22 out and Leonard took the shotgun. We walked over the bridge and along the side of the road behind the trees for about a hundred feet. We stopped near the road and jumped over a ditch and looked through a gap in a patch of pines.

From there we could see a grown up pasture and about a hundred yards out, a long low aluminum shed. It had two large double doors on it. One set of doors was wide open. I could see the Ultra-light Donny had mentioned. I had been up in one once, a two-seater. I was the passenger. It was like riding in a winged lawn mower.

The SUV was parked near the shed.

If Smoke Stack and Stumpy were going out of there in the Ultra-light, then there wouldn't be any room for Brett and Kelly. They'd either leave them, or pop them. I suspected the latter. But they hadn't done it yet because I could see Brett and Kelly by the shed. It looked as if they might be wearing handcuffs; their hands were tucked behind their backs and they were leaning against the building. The only way into the pasture, which was fenced with barbed wire, was over a cattle guard.

Smoke Stack and Stumpy were tugging the Ultra-light out of the shed.

"Looks like they aren't going to bother with a car," Leonard said.

"Go start the car," I said.

"You can shoot from here."

"I can. But I'm going through the trees and through the fence, and I'm going to walk straight toward them. I need to be closer and surer. You drive over that cattle guard like your ass is on fire, distract them. I'll take my shot then. It'll be Smoke Stack first. Then I reload and it's the other one."

"That's slow reloading with all that's going on, you and that single shot squirrel rifle," Leonard said.

"I'm quick and it's a little late to upgrade."

Leonard walked back to the car and I started through the trees and through the wire. I heard the car engine start. It wasn't loud enough to startle anyone, far back as he was. And then I heard the car coming, like the proverbial bat out of hell.

I hurried across the pasture. Smoke Stack hadn't seen me yet. He was preoccupied with another part of his plan. He hadn't wanted to share the two-seater at all. And I knew why. All that money from the previous heist had to have a place to rest.

He had an automatic pistol drawn, and he turned and shot his partner right through the head. I saw him heave something in a bag into the Ultra-light, then he started over toward Brett and Kelly, the automatic hanging from his hand. He was partially hidden by the Ultra-light. I could only get glimpses of him through the wings and the motor and the seating. He hadn't seen me yet. He was preoccupied.

I stopped and dropped to one knee and took my shot.

I saw his hair lift a little, my shot was so close.

But I missed. I NEVER FUCKING MISSED. And I had missed.

My heart sunk.

Smoke Stack wheeled. And when he did, Brett jumped up, and with her hands against her back, she leaped at him, hit him with a body slam and knocked him spinning backwards, his gun flying from his hand. I dropped the .22 and started running toward him. Leonard was flying through the cattle guard then, bearing down on Smoke Stack.

Smoke Stack got up and out from under Brett who struggled to her feet and tried to jump at him again. But Smoke Stack dodged her like a quarterback on the run and leapt into the Ultra-light. I heard the motor start up and a moment later the machine was bouncing over the field. I was running on a collision course with Leonard. He slammed on the brakes and I slid over the hood and jumped in on the other side.

"Go," I said.

The Ultra-light was gaining some speed. Its bounces were becoming higher. In a moment it would hop and then leap to the sky.

But the motor on that thing wasn't a match for a car. We were closing. As we passed Brett, who had struggled to her feet, she looked at me.

I waved.

The car bounced along until it was almost even with the Ultra-light. I hung myself out of the open window, eased out until I was sitting on the edge of it with my legs dangling, my arms inside, keeping me lodged. And then I eased an arm out.

"Closer," I said.

Leonard did that. I cocked one foot up until it was on the window support, and I shoved off just as the Ultra-light was making its big jump.

I hit the wing of the Ultra-light, scrambling for a grip, and my weight nodded it toward the ground. The wing hit. The propeller gnawed at the pasture. There was a sudden whirl as the sky came down and then went up again, followed by a close look at, and a hard impact with, the ground.

I heard a noise like someone dragging a rake through gravel. It was the Ultra-light spinning in circles like a confused idiot. The money had come loose of the bag and some of it was spinning in the air and some had been caught in the propeller and chopped up. It looked like the last hurrah of a parade, the last bits of confetti thrown.

On my feet, I saw Smoke Stack coming toward me. He was so angry he was actually foaming at the mouth. His face was scratched up.

"Now you get your shot, buddy," I said.

"I'll fucking kill you."

He was like a locomotive. It wasn't like that night in his house. He was crazed with anger and maybe he had been on drugs, or most likely had just underestimated me. That happens a lot. But he was dead serious now.

I dodged his rush and kicked out. I was trying to hit him in the solar plexus, but he instinctively crunched his body, and took the shot on his upraised forearms. The impact, the disorientation of the crash, had me off a bit, so the impact of hitting him like that knocked me down. He leaped on me like a big frog.

I heard Leonard slam the car door and start over. But me and Smoke Stack were into it. I spread my legs and got him between them. He tried to hit me. I put up my arms. I was deflecting most of the blows, but I was taking some of it. Finally I cupped one of his arms at the elbow and swung a leg to the side of his neck. I was trying to pull him into a triangle choke, but the angle wasn't right. He pushed my leg back so that it was being mashed across my face. It was damn uncomfortable. I used my other leg to kick at his hip, knocking him back a bit, loosening him. It allowed me to swing my leg free. I poked him in the eyes with my fingers, and when he went back and put a hand to his face, I rolled out from under him.

Now I was on my feet, where I preferred to be. I saw Leonard leaning against the car, the shotgun lying on the fender.

"You got him," Leonard said.

Smoke Stack came in swinging. I ducked him and came up with an upper cut that knocked him back. I kicked him in the nuts then, but he was too high on adrenaline for it to matter. He came swinging again. I glanced the blows off my forearms and got inside and grabbed his head and kneed him inside of the leg. Adrenaline wasn't enough to stop that pain.

His leg went out from under him. I swung a downward right cross, and back he went. He rolled onto his hands and knees and scuttled and finally got to his feet. He put a hand to his pocket, and when he brought it out, he had a knife.

He crouched, eased toward me. There was a sound like a cannon going off and Smoke Stack's head disappeared in a blur of red and gray and flying white fragments. Within a blink of an eye, what was left of him was lying on the ground.

I looked at Leonard. He was lowering the shotgun.

"You proved your point, and you got your licks in," he said. "But that knife, that could have been a problem."

WE FOUND THAT Brett and Kelly's hands were bound with plastic cuffs. We cut those off. I said to Brett, "You all right, baby?"

"Yeah," Brett said. "I'm fine. All they did was get an unauthorized look at my nubile body. A look like they got, I should have been paid money."

I grinned at her and we kissed.

I walked back and got the .22. The shell casing was still in it.

We packed up and drove out of there in Leonard's car, left the money and the bodies.

IT WAS A few weeks later.

A tip had led the police to the bodies in the field. Way it looked was there had been a problem between thieves. Smoke Stack had shot his partner and tried to escape, but crashed. Someone had blown his head off. They took this to be another partner. They were glad to get most of the money back. I don't know about the shredded stuff. I envisioned some bank clerk gluing the pieces back together like an archeologist reuniting shards of pottery. It was a silly thought, but it hung in my head.

The other partner, of course, wouldn't be found. Neither would the .22 that killed the two would-be robbers in the bank lot. The cops had an idea that one of the partners went rogue, first with a .22, then a shotgun. It was a silly theory, but thank goodness they liked that story and were sticking to it. They're not dumb, just arrogant.

It was a nice afternoon with a clear sky and a light wind. We were in the backyard grilling burgers, me and Brett and Leonard. The doorbell rang. That would be our guests.

I went through the house and let Marvin and Kelly and Donny in, walked them out back.

Leonard was flipping the burgers.

We greeted each other, talked.

Donny said, "I haven't said nothing, and I never will."

"I believe you," I said.

"I wouldn't want you mad at me," Donny said.

"That's good thinking," Leonard said.

"But I wouldn't say anyway. I…I can't thank you guys enough. You hadn't done what you did, I'd be dead."

"Absolutely," Leonard said.

"Thanks again for saving my little brother," Kelly said, "and thanks for passing on the payment I owed you guys. I can use the dough."

"Man," Leonard said. "You're the hero. You put yourself on the line. Changed your life, got your ass whipped by me, and thoroughly, I might add, and then you didn't even have any protection from those guys and still you went to work."

"You warned me," Kelly said. "You told me not to stay on the job."

"Yep," Leonard said. "We did."

"And, I sort of squealed when they put those cigarettes on me. I thought I could take it. I was sure I could. One burn and I was already starting to loosen my tongue."

"It hurts," Leonard said. "You're not a professional tough guy. We don't begrudge you trying to make the pain stop. Besides, in the long run it worked out."

"Well," Brett said, stretching out in a lawn chair, her long legs poking sweetly out of her shorts. "All's well that ends well and doesn't make a mess on the rug."

"Hear, hear," Marvin said.

"You said it right, Brett," Donny said. "They were hyenas. And I don't want to be like that."

"Good thinking," Brett said.

"I find a woman I care about," Donny said, "I hope she's half the woman you are, Brett."

"Oh, honey," Brett said smiling. "That's so sweet. But too optimistic. You can't find anyone half as good as me. A quarter of my worth maybe, if you're having a good day. But half, don't be silly."

THE BOY
WHO
BECAME
INVISIBLE

THE PLACE WHERE I grew up was a little town called Marvel Creek. Not much happened there that is well remembered by anyone outside of the town. But things went on, and what I'm aware of now is how much things really don't change. We just know more than we used to because there are more of us, and we have easier ways to communicate excitement and misery than in the old days.

Marvel Creek was nestled along the edge of the Sabine River, which is not a wide river, and as rivers go, not that deep, except in rare spots, but it is a long river, and it winds all through East Texas. Back then there were more trees than now, and where wild animals ran, concrete and houses shine bright in the sunlight.

Our little school wasn't much, and I hated going. I liked staying home and reading books I wanted to read, and running the then considerable woods and fishing the creeks for crawdads. Summers and after-noons and weekends I did that with my friend Jesse. I knew Jesse's parents lived differently than we did, and though we didn't have money, and would prob-ably have been called poor by the standards of the early sixties, Jesse's family still lived out on a farm where they used an outhouse and plowed with mules, raised most of the food they ate, drew water from a well, but curiously, had electricity and a big tall TV antennae that sprouted beside their house and could be adjusted for better reception by reaching through the living room window and turning it with a twist of the hands. Jesse's dad was quick to use the razor strop on Jesse's butt and back for things my parents would have thought unimportant, or at worst, an offense that required words, not blows.

Jesse and I liked to play Tarzan, and we took turns at it until we finally both decided to be Tarzan, and ended up being Tarzan twins. It was a great mythology we created and we ran the woods and climbed trees, and on Saturday we watched Jungle Theater at my house, which showed, if we were lucky, Tarzan or Jungle Jim movies, and if not so lucky, Bomba movies.

About fifth grade there was a shift in dynamics. Jesse's poverty began to be an issue for some of the kids at school. He brought his lunch in a sack, since he couldn't afford the cafeteria, and all his clothes came from the Salvation Army. He arrived at history class one morning wearing socks with big S's on them, which stood for nothing related to him, and they immediately became the target of James Willeford and Ronnie Kenn. They made a remark about how the S stood for Sardines, which would account for how Jesse smelled, and sadly, I remember thinking at that age that was a pretty funny crack until I looked at Jesse's slack, white face and saw him tremble beneath that patched Salvation Army shirt.

Our teacher came in then, Mr. Waters, and he caught part of the conversation. He said, "Those are nice socks, you got there, Jesse. Not many people can have monogrammed socks. It's a sign of sophistication, something a few around here lack."

It was a nice try, but I think it only made Jesse feel all the more miserable, and he put his head down on his desk and didn't lift it the entire class, and Mr. Waters didn't say a word to him. When class was over, Jesse was up and out, and as I was leaving, Mr. Waters caught me by the arm. "I saw you laughing when I came in. You've been that boy's friend since the two of you were knee high to a legless grasshopper."

"I didn't mean to," I said. "I didn't think."

"Yeah, well, you ought to."

That hit me pretty hard, but I'm ashamed to say not hard enough.

I DON'T KNOW when it happened, but it got so when Jesse came over I found things to do. Homework, or some chore around the house, which was silly, because unlike Jesse, I didn't really have any chores. In time he quit stopping by, and I would see him in the halls at school, and we'd nod at each other, but seldom speak.

The relentless picking and nagging from James and Ronnie continued, and as they became interested in girls, it increased. And Marilyn Townsend didn't help either. She was a lovely young thing and as cruel as they were.

One day, Jesse surprised us by coming to the cafeteria with his sack lunch. He usually ate outside on one of the stoops, but he came in this day and sat at a table by himself, and when Marilyn went by he watched her, and when she came back with her tray, he stood up and smiled, politely asked if she would like to sit with him.

She laughed. I remember that laugh to this day. It was as cold as a knife blade in the back and easily as sharp. I saw Jesse's face drain until it was white, and she went on by laughing, not even saying a word, just laughing, and pretty soon everyone in the place was laughing, and Marilyn came by me, and she looked at me, and heaven help me, I saw those eyes of hers and those lips, and whatever made all the other boys jump did the same to me...and I laughed.

Jesse gathered up his sack and went out.

I T WAS AT this point that James and Ronnie came up with a new approach. They decided to treat Jesse as if he were a ghost, as if he were invisible. We were expected to do the same. So as not to be mean to Jesse, but being careful not to burn my bridges with the in-crowd, I avoided him altogether. But there were times, here and there, when I would see him walking down the hall, and on the rare occasions when he spoke, students pretended not to hear him, or James would respond with some remark like, "Do you hear a duck quacking?"

When Jesse spoke to me, if no one was looking, I would nod.

This went on into the ninth grade, and it became such a habit, it was as if Jesse didn't exist, as if he really were invisible. I almost forgot about him, though I did note in math class one day there were stripes of blood across his back, seeping through his old worn shirt. His father and the razor strop. Jesse had nowhere to turn.

One afternoon I was in the cafeteria, just about to get in line, when Jesse came in carrying his sack. It was the first time he'd been in the cafeteria since the incident with Marilyn some time before. I saw him come in, his head slightly down, walking as if on a mission. As he came near me, for the first time in a long time, for no reason I can explain, I said, "Hi, Jesse."

He looked up at me surprised, and nodded, the way I did to him in the hall, and kept walking.

There was a table in the center of the cafeteria, and that was the table James and Ronnie and Marilyn had claimed, and as Jesse came closer, for the first time in a long time, they really saw him. Maybe it was because they were surprised to see him and his paper sack in a place he hadn't been in ages. Or maybe they sensed something. Jesse pulled a small revolver from his sack and before anyone knew what was happening, he fired three times, knocking all three of them to the floor. The place went nuts, people running in all directions. Me, I froze.

Then, like a soldier, he wheeled and marched back my way. As he passed me, he turned his head, smiled, said, "Hey, Hap," then he was out the door. I wasn't thinking clearly, because I turned and went out in the hall behind him, and the history teacher, Mr. Waters, saw him with the gun, said something, and the gun snapped again, and Waters went down. Jesse walked all the way to the double front door, which was flung wide open at that time of day, stepped out into the light and lifted the revolver. I heard it pop and saw his head jump and he went down. My knees went out from under me and I sat down right there in the hall, unable to move.

WHEN THEY WENT out to tell his parents what had happened to him, that Marilyn was disfigured, Ronnie wounded, and James and Mr. Waters were dead, they discovered them in bed where Jesse had shot them in their sleep.

The razor strop lay across them like a dead snake.